YOKO & FRIENDS
★ ★
SCHOOL DAYS

When I Grow Up

Text and jacket art by
Rosemary Wells

Interior illustrations by
Jody Wheeler

Hyperion Books for Children
New York

Printed in the United States of America

First Edition
1 3 5 7 9 10 8 6 4 2

LIBRARY OF CONGRESS CATALOGING-IN-PUBLICATION DATA
Wells, Rosemary.
When I grow up / text and jacket art by Rosemary Wells; interior illustrations by
Jody Wheeler.
p.   cm. — (Yoko & friends—school days)
Summary: The students in Mrs. Jenkins's class explore the careers they'd like to
have when they grow up, including Yoko who wants to be a Japanese teacher.
ISBN 0-7868-0731-8 (hc.) — ISBN 0-7868-1537-X (pbk.)
[1. Occupations—Fiction. 2. Schools—Fiction. 3. Cats—Fiction. 4. Animals—
Fiction. 5. Japanese Americans—Fiction.] I. Wheeler, Jody, ill. II. Title.
PZ7.W46843 Wf 2003
[E]—dc21
2001057508

Visit www.hyperionchildrensbooks.com

"Monday morning, we will start

When I Grow Up week,

boys and girls," said Mrs. Jenkins.

"Who will go first?" asked Claude.

"I will call on you in

al-pha-bet-i-cal order,"

said Mrs. Jenkins.

"I will be first!" said Claude.

"I will start at the end of the

alphabet," said Mrs. Jenkins.

"Yoko will be first!" said Grace.

worried

"What are you going to wear

for When I Grow Up week?"

Timothy asked Yoko.

"I don't know," said Yoko.

puzzled

"One day," said Timothy, "I will be a fireman. So I will dress up in a fireman's hat and slicker."

"I want to be a honey farmer," said Nora. "So I will dress up in a beekeeper's hat and suit."

6

"I'm going to be a policeman,"

said Claude.

"I am going to be a ballerina!"

said Grace.

"We are going be chefs!" said
the Franks. "We will cook only
franks and beans!"

No one knew what Yoko
would be.

Yoko sat very quietly on the school bus.

All the way home, she thought about what she would be when she grew up.

"You can be anything you want, my little cherry blossom," said Yoko's mother. "You can be a doctor, someday."

"I don't like germs," said Yoko.

"You could be an artist," said Yoko's mother.

"I am better at music," said Yoko.

"You could be a teacher," said

Yoko's mother.

"But teachers don't dress up,"

said Yoko.

"Oh, yes they do," said Yoko's

mother. "Teachers dress up

in Japan."

"Then I will be a Japanese

teacher!" said Yoko.

Yoko's mother dressed Yoko up in her fancy kimono.

She put on Yoko's special obi.

She gave Yoko her special golden fan.

"I need something else," said Yoko.

"What do you need, my little

cherry blossom?" asked Yoko's

mother.

"I need someone to teach," said

Yoko. "I want to teach

the Net-su-ke family."

"Oh!" said Yoko's mother. "The Netsuke family is very precious. You cannot take them to school."

"Please?" said Yoko. "I will be very, very careful."

"You must be very, very careful,"
said Yoko's mother, "and bring
them right home. Everyone may
look, but no one may touch the
Netsuke family, because they
belonged to your great-great-
grandmother."

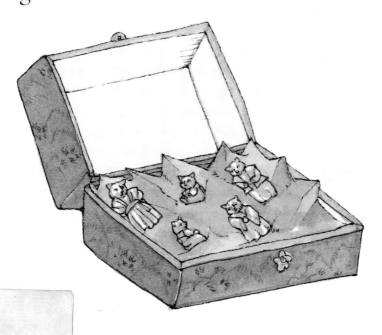

15

Yoko wrapped each member of
the Netsuke family in special
paper.

Monday morning, she put on her
kimono.

Her mother helped her with the
obi.

Yoko took the fan and the
Netsuke family on the bus in a
special bag.

Mrs. Jenkins asked, "Yoko, will you
be the first to tell us and show us
what you want to be when you
grow up?"

Yoko said, "I want to be a teacher
when I grow up.

"I will teach Japanese to people
from America.

I will teach English to people from
Japan."

Yoko unwrapped the Netsuke
family.

She lined them up on

Mrs. Jenkins's desk.

"These are my first students.

They are very old. They belonged

to my great-great-grandmother

in Japan."

"Oooooooooooh!"

said everybody.

Everybody wanted to hold

and touch the Netsuke family.

"We can only look at them, boys

and girls!" said Mrs. Jenkins.

Everyone crowded around the

desk.

"I want them!" said somebody.

Yoko wrapped the Netsuke family in their special paper and put them in their special bag. She put the bag and her fan in her cubby.

"I wish you the best of luck in
your career, Yoko!"
said Mrs. Jenkins.

Timothy went next.

He showed everyone his fire

hatchet and his fire hose.

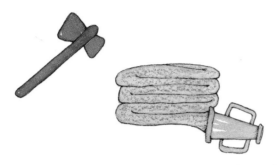

After lunch, Nora put on her bee

coat and her bee hat and told the

class about bee farming.

wer → Bee → Honey

At school-bus time, everyone went

to their cubbies to get their things.

Yoko looked in her cubby. Her fan

was there, but the Netsuke family

was gone!

Yoko cried all the way home on the school bus.

She cried all the way through dinner.

Yoko's mother cried, too.

"How can anyone take something

that belongs to someone else?"

asked Yoko's mother.

That night, somebody opened the

Netsuke bag.

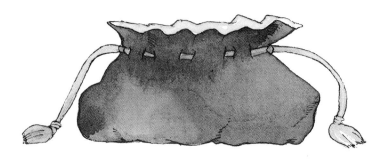

Somebody unwrapped the

Netsuke family.

Somebody took them to bed.

But no one else knew who it was.

Mrs. Jenkins tried to find out.

But no one would tell.

Yoko cried.

Everybody looked at Yoko.

Timothy tried to make her feel
better.

But Yoko did not feel better.

One person in the class knew where the Netsuke family was. That person almost cried, too. Instead, that person brought the Netsuke family in to school very early the next morning, and put them on Yoko's desk.

Yoko could not believe her eyes.

She unwrapped the paper.

No one was broken. No one was

chipped.

"Who did it?" asked Timothy.

"Who took them?" asked Charles.

"I don't know," said Yoko.

But in the bottom of the bag was

a little candy valentine heart.

It said, *I'm sorry!*

"And that's what counts!"

said Yoko.

Dear Parents,

When our children were young we lived in a small house, but we always made a space just for books. When their dad or I would read a story out loud, the TV was always off—radio and music, too—because it intruded.

Soon this peaceful half hour of every day became like a little island vacation. Our children are lifetime readers now with an endless curiosity for the rich world waiting between the covers of good books. It cost us nothing but time well spent and a library card.

This set of easy-to-read books is about the real nitty-gritty of elementary school. There are new friends, and bullies, too. There are germs and the "Clean Hands" song, new ways of painting pictures, learning music, telling the truth, gossiping, teasing, laughing, crying, separating from Mama, scary Halloweens, and secret valentines. The stories are all drawn from the experiences my children had in school.

It's my hope that these books will transport you and your children to a setting that's familiar, yet new. And that it will prove to be a place where you can explore the exciting new world of school together.